The Magnificent Misfits and the Great Mistake

J.J. MURHALL

Illustrated by
Eleanor Taylor

BLOOMSBURY
CHILDREN'S
BOOKS

This book is dedicated to
Michael and Saoirse Ruby,
and to all those 'misfits'
I have ever known,
including the most 'magnificent'
one of all – Alfie.

XX

First published in Great Britain in 1998
Bloomsbury Publishing Plc, 38 Soho Square, London, W1V 5DF

The moral right of the author has been asserted
A CIP catalogue record of this book is available from the
British Library

ISBN 0 7475 3639 2

Printed in England by Clays Ltd, St Ives plc

10 9 8 7 6 5 4 3 2 1

Cover design by Michelle Redford

One

'Seymour Potts! Have you finally gone stark staring bonkers, boy?' Mr Spittle, the PE teacher, could hardly contain himself as he jumped up and down jabbing his whistle at a tall, gangly boy with a mass of flaming red curly hair. 'Because only you could be responsible for this ridiculous eyesore.' He pointed a shaky finger across the playing fields of St Gregorys towards the goalposts, which had been draped in masses of streamers and balloons.

It was a hot July afternoon, but great black storm clouds had now gathered and a strong wind had suddenly whipped up, making the streamers flutter out in all directions. It seemed more like a winter's

evening now than two thirty on a
summer's afternoon.

'This isn't a party, Potts,' hissed Mr
Spittle, putting his face within inches of
Seymour's. His wispy strands of hair blew
over his face like a curtain and he angrily
smoothed them back across his shiny bald
head. His breath stank of the cheese and
onion pie that had been chucked on to the

plates at lunchtime. It was disgusting, but Seymour didn't flinch. Mr Spittle was a bad-breathed balding bully and he would never back down to one of those.

'This happens to be a very serious football match against Bracknell,' continued the teacher, crimson with rage,

'which is why the whole school is being allowed to watch. And you and your no-good friends could do with taking a few lessons from some of St Gregorys' star pupils.' His eyes narrowed. 'Why must you make light of everything, Potts? Life is not one long party.'

'Well I rather like to think that it is, sir,' replied Seymour brightly. 'You see, I believe that if everyone smiled and tried to enjoy themselves a bit more, the world would be a much happier place. Lemon Bonbon, sir?' He pulled a crumpled bag of dusty sweets from his trouser pocket and held them right under Mr Spittle's twitchy nose.

'Are you trying to be *funny*, Potts?' he muttered slowly. A light layer of foam had formed in the teacher's mouth and was now frothing on his lower lip.

'Funny, sir? I do hope so, sir!' replied Seymour cheerfully.

Then before Mr Spittle bubbled over with rage, a delicate-looking boy with jet black hair and big dark eyes leant across and brushed the teacher's mouth lightly with a tissue.

'Ugh! I can't bare dribble,' said Fabian Farquar distastefully. 'Dribbling is for dogs and babies. And I certainly don't like either of those slobbery creatures very much.'

Fabian was Seymour's best friend and they, along with Keith and Timothy Elastic, Barrington Small and Seymour's younger sister Elsie, were standing with Seymour, waiting for kick-off. They were some distance away from the rest of the spectators. This was because Seymour

Potts and his gang were considered to be the oddest children in the whole school. They never quite fitted in. They were always the ones who got the simplest answers wrong during lessons, or came up with ridiculous scatterbrained solutions to science problems. They were frequently caught staring dreamily out of the classroom window. They did some very strange things as well, especially Seymour. He once brought his pet goldfish to school in a rucksack filled with water, because he thought it might be feeling lonely. In fact, they always seemed to be in some sort of trouble and Mr Spittle loathed them all. He wished the school taught only the likes of Nathan Best, Steven Riley, Joshua Smug and the highly-talented Julian and Colin Crane brothers. They were St Gregorys' finest. Great at sport. Even better at maths. Top at this. Top at that. IQs that went hurtling through the ceiling.

Mr Spittle sighed wistfully as he

watched the brawny brainboxes run on to the pitch. 'Model pupils each and every one,' he mumbled to himself. Then he glared back at Seymour and the others.

'As for you lot,' he spat, his voice filled with venom. 'You'd better stay out of my way. You're a bunch of no-hopers and if I could, I'd have you all expelled. You've about as much chance of making something of yourselves as flying to Mars.' With that, he blew shrilly on his whistle and jogged off to start the match as another gust of wind almost knocked the children off their feet.

It was ten minutes into the match when the storm really began to take hold. The rain poured down in barrel loads and soon the pitch was awash with brown muddy water. The game was abandoned and everyone ran to the changing-rooms and the school hall for shelter.

Seymour and his mates stopped and waited for Elsie to catch up. She looked

like a little drowned mouse scurrying towards them with her pure white hair plastered to her head. Elsie could barely run against the wind and she gripped tightly on to Gladys' hand. Gladys was her imaginary friend who never left her side.

Up ahead, Nathan Best and his super-brainy friends pulled frantically at the changing-room door. Someone appeared to have locked it. Suddenly, there was an almighty clap of thunder and a flash of brilliant lightening which lit up the sky and bounced off Elsie's glasses.

'Hurry, sis!' cried Seymour urgently. He was getting soaked. As Elsie caught up with him, the reflection in her glasses gradually began to change as the whole sky turned a vivid shade of green. Nathan Best and the super-brains cowered against the changing-room door, watching, aghast, as Seymour and his friends were enveloped by the luminous glow.

Seymour stared up into the sky. It was hard to see at first through the driving rain, but, wiping his dripping face, he glimpsed a distinctive shape between the storm clouds. Seymour turned his head to one side and saw to his amazement that way up in the sky a huge eye was staring straight back down at him. It blinked once, and then it was gone.

*

It was Barrington Small who got sucked up first. Despite his name, Barrington was a large boy, but the force was so great it left his muddy shoes behind. As he went hurtling up into the sky, he was closely followed by the Elastic twins, Fabian and Seymour and finally Elsie, her hand stretched out behind her, still holding on to Gladys. The noise was tremendous, it sounded like someone was sucking the world's largest milkshake through the world's narrowest straw. Nathan Best and his friends could only gaze, open-mouthed, as the figures became smaller and smaller and finally disappeared between the clouds, along with the streamers and balloons which had previously flown behind the goalposts in a riot of colour.

A few moments later, the rain stopped and the sun burst through to reveal a bright blue sky. When Mr Spittle, who had been sheltering in the school hall, came jogging around the corner, all that could be seen on the pitch was a solitary balloon floating above the clouds.

'Ah. There you are, boys,' he declared in a friendly manner that he saved for his favourite pupils. 'We're going to restart the match now the weather's picked up.'

The five faces stared up at him, unable to speak.

'Whatever's up? You look like you've seen a ghost. Talking of strange creatures, you haven't seen Seymour Potts, have you? Only I've just reported him to the headmaster for defacing the goalposts.'

Steven Riley pointed a shaky finger towards the sky. 'Flown away. Flown away,' he mumbled.

Mr Spittle frowned. It was unlike the fantastic high-jump champion of St Gregorys to talk such complete and utter nonsense.

'Are you feeling all right, Riley? Maybe you'd better go and have a lie down. I don't know where Potts and his friends have got to,' he said, polishing his whistle vigorously on his shorts, 'but I hope for their sakes it's somewhere out of my sight,' and he jogged briskly off to the pitch. Halfway across he stopped, bent down and gingerly picked up a pair of muddy shoes.

'And to *whom* do these monstrosities

belong? How *dare* they clutter up my playing field,' he roared, shaking them around by their laces.

'They belong to Barrington Small, sir,' replied Nathan Best, his face still white with shock.

Mr Spittle's eyes narrowed and he nodded his head. 'Barrington birdbrain Small. I might have guessed. Well when I catch up with him he'll be flying through the school gates on the end of *my* shoe.'

'You're too late, sir,' replied Colin Crane with a shrug. 'He and his friends have already gone. I wouldn't be at all surprised if they weren't halfway to the moon by now.'

Two

'*What the? Who the? How the?*' Omonoslomo,
ruler of at least seventeen planets, and the
chief executive of intergalactic spaceship
parking, paced the room, his long flowing
robes sweeping across the vast marble
floor. In his hand he held five glossy
photographs showing the fresh faces of
Nathan Best and his super-brainy mates.

'*These* were the children I wanted!' he
roared, waving them towards a robot who
was whirring around the floor after him.
'When word gets out that I've picked the
wrong children to become the new World
Warriors, I'll be lucky if I can get a job
sweeping up meteorite debris on that
awful planet Swampsack.'

He flopped down into his big wing-backed chair and sighed deeply. 'Things are not looking good, Pickthank,' he said, shaking his head and scratching his long bushy beard. 'It was bad enough when they assembled you at the robot cash 'n' carry, and I became the laughing stock of the annual Masters of the Universe convention, without the added humiliation of this catastrophe.'

Pickthank stood in front of Omonoslomo's desk whirring quietly. It had to be said, as robots go, he was a bit of a mess. One of his arms was shorter than the other. His head was much bigger than his body, with tufts of wire sticking out of the top of it, and every now and then great plumes of strange-smelling blue smoke would waft out of the back of his welded-on tin underpants.

Suddenly, the big gold telephone beside Omonoslomo began to ring, and he paled visibly. This was the hotline to Dr K's headquarters. Dr K was the oldest and most powerful Master of planets way beyond the solar system. He also happened to be in charge of the hiring and firing of all superheroes throughout the universe, including the World Warriors who, as stated in *The Bumper Guide To Superheroes* Vol. 13, mustn't be any younger than eight and strictly no older than thirteen.

Omonoslomo snatched up the phone. 'Dr K. How are you, sir?' he asked a little too brightly. 'Have I brought in the new World Warriors yet? Why yes, sir. Of course, sir. They're waiting in the arrival chamber now. We gave the old ones a really good send-off, and Pickthank baked them a cake with candles for every year that they'd been a superhero. It was very touching.'

Omonoslomo picked up the photograph of Nathan Best looking tanned and lovely. How could he have made such a stupid mistake?

'I chose some children of the earth from a country called Engerland this time,' continued Omonoslomo, trying to sound convincing. 'E N G E R L A N D, sir!' he repeated, bellowing into the mouthpiece and rolling his eyes. Dr K may well be a mighty ruler, but he really could do with cleaning out his ears.

'You've never heard of it? Well, sir, it's a

small island about the size of your bath.'
Omonoslomo put the receiver down beside
him while Dr K droned on, and tapped a
description of Seymour and his friends
into the computer.

After a moment, reams of paper began to
roll out of it. Then it began to wail like a
siren and the words

REJECT!
REJECT!
REJECT!

flashed urgently up on the screen.

Omonoslomo picked up the phone
again. 'Sorry, sir. I had to answer the door
to the pizza delivery alien,' he lied, staring
at the screen in amazement. 'Oh. You want
to know what the children are like? Well.
They're brilliant, sir. The very best I could
find. I *know* you've got your reputation as
superhero selector to consider, but believe
me this lot are *something else*. In fact, I'm
sure they'll be up there in the world-saving
league with legends like Superman and

those turtle things in no time at all. Anyway, must dash, my pizza's getting cold.' He slammed the phone down and flopped back into his chair.

'And if you believe that, cloth ears, you'll believe anything. Pickthank, my trusty, rusty robot, you'd better bring the little blighters in, I suppose.'

As Pickthank glided out of the room, Omonoslomo glanced up at the enormous eye-shaped TV screen that covered one vast wall of his office. Seymour and his mates could be seen standing in a large white room, looking extremely puzzled. Suddenly, Barrington's face loomed right up close to the screen, making Omonoslomo leap back in his chair. Barrington stared blankly and picked his nose.

'Great. That's all I need. A nose-picking superhero,' scoffed Omonoslomo. Then he waited despondently for Pickthank to return with the children. The lives of

Seymour Potts and his friends were
about to be changed forever.

'What do you mean 'Welcome to the planet
Twart?' demanded Fabian Farquar, looking
most annoyed. 'Is this some kind of joke,
you overgrown baked-bean can?'

'You must follow me. You have been
sucked up here as the chosen ones,' replied
Pickthank politely.

'Will this take long?' asked Barrington,

following the little robot and wrinkling his nose up at the funny smell that wafted out of him. 'Only my gran's cooking me pie and chips tonight, and I told her I wouldn't be late home. I'll be in trouble for losing my shoes as it is.' He stared forlornly down at his big bare feet.

'As World Warriors you will have no need of this thing you call the *pie* and the *chips*,' said Pickthank, leading the children through a revolving door and into Omonoslomo's office. 'You will be too busy guarding your planet from the forces of evil to think of such things. Master O, I have brought the new children,' he announced, leading them up to the enormous desk.

Omonoslomo swung around in his chair looking more than a little cross. Seymour gave him an extra-friendly smile, but Omonoslomo just glared back at him.

'I, Omonoslomo, ruler of at least seventeen planets, have made a terrible mistake in choosing you to become the new World Warriors,' said Omonoslomo, looking at each child in turn.

Barrington put up his hand. 'Er. Excuse me, Mr Omo, but what's a World Worrier? Is it someone who worries all the time? Because I worry a lot, you see. About where I've put my socks, or whether I've got my times table right. So I think I might be quite good, I've had loads of practice.'

Omonoslomo ignored him. 'I have looked you up on the computer that lists all of the children throughout the universe alphabetically and in order of intelligence, and I can honestly say that you lot came out as the worst contenders *ever*.' He picked up a sheet of paper and read out loud:

'*Seymour Potts. Aged ten. Hobbies include collecting stamps.*' He peered at Seymour over the top of it. 'Well, that's not *so* bad, I suppose. Boring, but fairly popular on planet earth, I understand.'

'Um. I think that should read *ants*, actually,' replied Seymour.

'I collect *ants*, not stamps. I'm building a block of flats for them out of matchsticks. I'm on the third floor already, only my mum's given up smoking so it's harder to get the matches now. I have to wait for my Uncle Charlie to come round 'cause he smokes like a chimney. I also collect stones, but only grey or white ones, and the

wheels off toy cars, and sweet wrappers for wallpapering my bedroom with.' Seymour smiled at Omonoslomo proudly.

'But don't you have any *normal* hobbies?' asked Omonoslomo hopefully, 'like playing for the school football team or attending a chess club?'

Seymour shook his head. 'No – but I can recite the alphabet backwards,' he added brightly.

Omonoslomo sighed and glanced back down at the paper. *'Fabian Farquar. Aged nine. Son of famous parents who host daytime chat show on TV called 'Farquar Finds Out'.'* He looked up at Fabian who was busily cleaning his blazer.

'Hobbies include,' here Omonoslomo let out a cry of disbelief, *'visiting the launderette!!* What kind of hobby is *that?'*

Fabian cocked an eyebrow and replied haughtily. 'A very *clean* one, actually. I get a lot of pleasure from watching a tumble dryer go around and around and aro—'

'Thank you. I've heard quite enough,' interrupted Omonoslomo hastily. He frowned at the Elastic twins frowning back at him. *'Keith and Timothy Elastic. Aged eight and a half. Hobbies. Just one.* Moaning!'

'That's right,' replied Timothy, eager to have a moan before his brother. 'And let me tell you, I'm really fed up about being here. I'm missing all my favourite programmes on TV *and* I've probably missed my tea as well. And Mr and Mrs Checkocheck, that's the couple who adopted us because our mum and dad got so fed up with us moaning morning, noon and night, will be wondering where we are. By the time we get home we'll have to go straight to bed and *my* bed's *really* uncomfortable. It sags in the middle and the sheets are all scratchy, and—'

'Mine too,' interrupted Keith, 'and it takes ages to brush my teeth before I go to bed. It's *so boring*. I hate brushing my teeth, and having a bath. It's *so boring*. Soap stinks, doesn't it? And *my* bed's *really* uncomfortable as well and—'

'Stop!!' cried Omonoslomo, 'you're giving me a headache!' He ran his finger down the list. Barrington Small. The nose picker. At least he was big and hearty-looking, thought Omonoslomo desperately.

'*Barrington Small. Aged nine and a half,*' read Omonoslomo out loud. '*Hobbies: granny-sitting, cat-sitting and just plain sitting. Can also burp louder than any child in his school.*'

'Shall I give you a demonstration?' asked Barrington proudly.

'If you must,' replied Omonoslomo wearily.

Barrington took a few big gulps of air and let out an almighty burp. He sounded like a gorilla with wind, only twice as noisy.

Omonoslomo gave him a faint smile, and then saw with relief that he'd reached the last child on the list. *'Elsie Potts. Aged eight. No hobbies, as Gladys takes up most of her time.'*

Omonoslomo gave her a friendly smile. This kid was his last chance of finding someone half decent for the World Warrior job.

'Who's Gladys, my dear? An elderly aunt you have to visit? What a kind and considerate child. We encourage our World Warriors to be helpful, especially to the elderly.'

Elsie stepped forward, her hand outstretched. *'This* is Gladys,' she announced, pointing to the empty space beside her. 'She's my best friend and she sleeps in my wardrobe.'

Pickthank hurried over and shook the imaginary Gladys' hand enthusiastically. 'She's very pretty,' he said to Elsie. 'I had a friend once that no one else could see. A robot called Marvin. Only one day he drifted off into space. Sometimes I see him floating past the window as he does another circuit of the universe. He always waves at me.' A rusty tear welled up in the robot's eye and he blew his bolt nose on a tin handkerchief.

'Oh, this is ridiculous!' shouted Omonoslomo, jumping out of his chair. Imaginary friends! Burping boys! *Ant* collectors! Washing machine fanatics! You

lot are nothing but a bunch of– of–'
Omonoslomo spluttered in frustration to
find the word. *'Misfits*!!' he finally roared.

The children looked nervously at each
other. They'd been called a lot of things in
their time, but never *misfits*.

Suddenly though, a smile began to
flicker across the mighty ruler's face.
'That's it!' he cried. 'I can tell Dr K that
Nathan Best and his friends got sucked
into a black hole on their way here. It was
a tragic accident. However! I did manage
to find *another* group of children. A bit
odd-looking, I agree, but superheroes in
the making, nevertheless.'

He looked at Seymour and the others
seriously. 'No longer will you be called
weirdo, dimbat or thicky. For you will
travel through the universe and guard
your planet as the world's newest fighting
force. It's a tough job, but hey, somebody's
got to do it.'

The children looked at each other

excitedly. Superheroes. Fighting force. *Universe* travellers! This was too much!

'Pickthank. Iron the uniforms and prepare the Power Powder,' ordered Omonoslomo. 'The World Warriors are no more. Make haste. Make way. Because today the *Magnificent Misfits* have arrived!'

Three

'What's happened to my school uniform?' asked Barrington, staring down at the bright pink stretchy suit he'd been told to put on. It was far too small for him and his big toe was poking through a hole in one of the feet. 'I've already lost my shoes today. What's my gran going to say when she sees me dressed up like this? She'll get the shock of her life.

'Your grandma will not recognise you,' replied Omonoslomo. 'In fact, no one will recognise you when you have your Misfit uniforms on.'

'Well, thank goodness for that,' scoffed Fabian, pulling at the seat of his extremely tight suit. 'I'll be the laughing stock of the launderette otherwise. I don't know *how* I'm going to keep the flipping thing clean, either. Fancy giving me a white one to wear. I'll be far too busy washing it to be able to do any superhero saving stuff.' He tutted loudly and brushed the front of his gleaming outfit fussily.

Seymour, Elsie and the Elastic twins didn't look any better, either. Seymour's suit sleeves were almost up to his elbows and the hood was rubbing under his chin, and Elsie's and the twins' suits were far too big.

'How can I be a superhero if I can't see where I'm going?' moaned Keith, trying to peer out from beneath the hood.

'Yeah. You could have given us ones that fitted properly,' added his brother. 'And I *really* hate purple,' he said, staring down crossly at his shiny mauve suit. 'What a horrible colour!'

'They're standard-sized superhero uniforms in this season's colours,' snapped

Omonoslomo, 'made to fit the likes of Nathan Best and other perfect-looking children. It's not my fault that you're not a standard size. As for your school uniforms, they've been sucked into a vortex. When you return to earth you will find them folded neatly on your beds along with your Miskits. A Miskit is a cunningly-disguised lunchbox that you will carry with you at all times. It contains

everything you need to guard the world from the evil Viles who will be heading towards earth any day now.'

Omonoslomo switched on the enormous eye-shaped TV, and a photograph filled the screen. It was of a man, one shot taken from the side, the other from the front. The children didn't know which angle looked worse, because he was certainly no oil painting.

He had a long thin face as sharp as a razor, big slab-like yellow teeth, a pointy beak of a nose and a glass eye like a blue marble, which followed you around the room. On his head he wore an orangey-blond wavy wig. He was wearing a brown jacket with enormous lapels and a washed-out yellow shirt with even bigger ones. Running up the front of it was a frill which had half his dinner spilt down it.

'Vile,' announced Omonoslomo gravely.

'Yes. He is rather revolting-looking, isn't he?' replied Elsie, shielding Gladys' eyes.

'No. That's his name,' said Omonoslomo, tapping the screen. 'Vince Vile. Also likes to be known as His Vileness, The Vile One, or Wily Vily. He is a master of disguise.' Omonoslomo flicked the switch, and various snapshots showed Vince dressed up as the Prime Minister, a bus conductor, a ballet dancer and even the Queen.

'Vile works with two others,' continued Omonoslomo. 'Their names are Lumpy and Gretch and they call themselves the Planet Cruisers. We have no clear pictures of them, as the planet Swampsack where they come from is the gloomiest, darkest place in the whole universe. But believe you me, they certainly wouldn't win any beauty contests, either.'

Seymour shuddered. He always thought aliens would look pretty horrible, but Vince Vile was far more hideous than anything with two heads and webbed feet.

'Vile is not your only enemy, though,' continued Omonoslomo, flicking the switch again. The children stared up at the screen. Staring back at them was a little old lady wearing little-old-lady-type clothes: sensible shoes, a woolly high-buttoned coat with a mangy fox-fur draped around her neck, thick brown tights, and a big fluffy hat that made her look as if a cat was asleep on her head. In one hand she held a large white handbag, and in the other a pull-along shopping bag on wheels. She looked as though she should be taking over Tescos, not the world.

'Flo Fancy,' announced Omonoslomo. 'The name she uses on earth, anyway. Her real name is Ma Vile, and she is Vince's granny. They loathe each other, and she wants to get her wrinkly old hands on the earth before Vince does. Ma Vile works alone, except for that thing around her neck. That's her pet fox, Graham. Don't be fooled by either of them. They are both highly dangerous, and that bag does *not* contain the weekly groceries, it harbours more dastardly gadgets than you're ever likely to see and she won't hesitate to use them, either. Come over to the window, I've something to show you.'

Omonoslomo led the children towards a big window and pulled back the curtains. Outside, the planet Twart could be seen, and the children gasped as they saw the pink sky, and the landscape stretching out before them. All the roads and pavements were built on towering stilts, and below, visible as far as the eye could see, was a barren expanse of desert. The roads coiled around each other like a gigantic Scalextric kit, and space ships of all shapes and sizes sped along the track honking their horns as they tackled a sharp bend, or took off in a cloud of dust on the sand below. And wherever they looked, they could see aliens with gigantic ears and four feet, robots, or people dressed like Omonoslomo, in long silky robes of various shades.

Seymour and his friends were amazed.
Surely this must be a dream! Omonoslomo
indicated towards the stars. In the far
distance was one that shone brighter than
all the others. Suddenly it went dark and
then lit up again.

'That's the planet Ghastly,' said
Omonoslomo, 'where the Viles come from.
It's hideous, just one big neon sign that
flashes on and off continuously day and
night. Apparently it's so bright and garish

41

you feel quite ill when you land on it. Next to it, about ten thousand light years away, is the planet Swampsack. Swampsack is guarded by an enormous vulture that looms over it on its perch. It casts a shadow so huge it blocks out nearly all of the light. Swampsack and Ghastly are both horrible places and I hope you never have to visit them.'

'So do I,' said Seymour nervously. 'Anyway, can't we go home now and start being the Magnificent Misfits? I'm quite looking forward to it.'

'I have one last thing to give you before you leave,' replied Omonoslomo, unlocking a steel cabinet. 'In here is the object that the World Warriors had to guard before they became too old for the job. You must do the same. If this ever gets into the wrong hands and is taken back to Ghastly or Swampsack, its power will be misused, and the most dreadful thing will happen. Children all over the world will wake up one day and find that they have turned into their parents – only the boys will be their mums and the girls, their dads! Their real parents will be rounded up and taken to Swampsack, where they will spend their days mowing the grass that grows an inch a minute, and avoiding the millions of crocodiles that roam freely around. And each day Swampsack is slowly shrinking, so eventually they will all fall off it.

'As for the children, they will be helpless to resist. They will have to wear their parents' clothes, the girls may even grow beards or moustaches. They must do their parents' job, wash, cook, clean and look after their baby brothers or sisters. There'll be no Christmas, birthdays or trips out. Just early to bed, and *extremely* early to rise. And any money that this new breed of 'Kidult' earns will go straight to the villainous Viles, who will rule with a rod of iron. '

The Magnificent Misfits couldn't believe
their ears. Elsie didn't fancy being her dad
at all. He had the most boring job and
wore the most terrible ties. Barrington
didn't want to wake up as his granny,
either. All she ever did was knit, play
bingo and hum to herself. The thought of
becoming any adult, let alone their
parents, was just too horrible for words.

'So what exactly do we have to keep safe

then?' asked Fabian, trying to get a glimpse of what was inside the cabinet. He hoped it was something exciting and worth guarding, like a jewel or a rare crystal. He was getting very hot and sticky inside his suit and couldn't wait to get home to give it a wash.

'*This* is what you must keep safe,' said Omonoslomo, turning around and holding the object very carefully in both hands. Everyone stared at it.

'Pickled onions!' declared Keith, looking really disappointed. 'How can a jar of pickled onions be powerful?'

'They may look ordinary,' replied Omonoslomo, handing the jar to Seymour, 'but these onions are the most powerful objects in the whole universe. They were found by Dr K as he was digging in his garden one day. He knew they were something really special because he had heard the rumours circulating around the universe about the strange and potent

Power of the Pickles that had been buried for a thousand and one years. Imagine his surprise when he stuck a spade into his flowerbed and stumbled upon such a treasure. And now you, the Magnificent Misfits, must keep them safe for him. But whatever you do, *don't* open the lid. And *don't* let the Viles near them. Now, it's time for you to depart.'

'How will we get home?' asked Barrington, staring at the pickles which were making him feel hungry. 'On the bus? Can you lend me the fare? I don't get my pocket money until the end of the week.'

'You will travel by space hoppers,' explained Omonoslomo, leading the Magnificent Misfits out into the strange pink glow of Twart. Leaning against a wall were six huge orange balls, each with two handles that looked like ears.

'I'm afraid we've had to make some cuts in the superhero transportation department,' said Omonoslomo.

'However, when you return to earth you can deflate your hoppers and they should fit neatly into your Miskits.'

The children stared down at the space hoppers and then across the sky towards the planets in the distance. Earth seemed a very long way away. Barrington was looking worried. He had trouble riding a bike, let alone a giant balloon.

'I am also giving each of you your own individual power that will start to work when you take your specially-prepared

Power Powder back on planet earth,' continued Omonoslomo. 'You will, of course, be able to do the usual superhero stuff, like jumping ten feet in the air whilst doing funny hand movements. This always seems totally pointless to me but I know you earth kids love all that kung fuey stuff. Seymour Misfit, you will soon have the power to hear over great distances. Fabian Misfit, you will have telescopic sight.'

'Oo, that's good,' said Fabian eagerly. 'Because I'm meant to go to the opticians next week. My mother thinks I might need glasses.'

'Barrington Misfit,' continued Omonoslomo, 'you will be very, very strong, and as agile as a cat. You will be able to jump higher than a house.' He glanced at Barrington standing there like a big pink blob. 'I hope,' he added hastily.

Barrington's face broke into a smile. 'I've always wanted to be good at sport,' he announced, bouncing up and down on his toes, 'only I was too big and clumsy. Not any more, though.' Suddenly he jumped into the air with his legs wide apart.

'*Aaaaayeee!!*' he cried, waving his arms in front of him like he'd seen them do on the TV. *Rrrippp!* went the seat of his suit as he landed with a thud. He stared forlornly at his Noddy print underpants hanging out of the hole at the back of his trousers.

'I'll go and get a needle and thread,' said Pickthank, hurrying off as Omonoslomo rolled his eyes in exasperation.

'Elsie Misfit,' Omonoslomo continued after a moment, 'you will be able to shout louder than anybody in the whole universe. And finally, Keith and Timothy Misfit. Both of you will now have the most amazing sense of smell.'

'The power to *smell*!' shouted Timothy, stamping his foot. 'What kind of power is *that*? It's not fair. Why can't we have great hearing like Seymour? Or that telescopic

thing that Fabian's been given? Whoever heard of a superhero going around *sniffing* things? It's bad enough normally, with all those nasty smells like the school canteen and the public toilets in the High Street. What's it going to be like now we've got super-noses?' He looked at his brother who nodded, tutted and sniffed loudly.

'You'll just have to make the most of it,' replied Omonoslomo firmly.

Pickthank returned with the needle and thread and sewed up Barrington's suit. It still looked as if it might split open again at any moment.

At last, the children were ready to depart. They boarded their space hoppers, switched on the ignition and revved them up.

'You push the ears forward to go faster and back to slow down,' explained Omonoslomo. He pointed towards a bright blue planet in the distance. 'That's the earth. Keep going straight ahead and you should be there in about twenty minutes.'

Omonoslomo patted Seymour on the back. 'Seymour Misfit, I'm putting you in charge. Don't let me down. Planet earth will be depending on you, so guard those onions with your life.'

Omonoslomo and Pickthank stepped back as the children revved up their engines again. Seymour was the first to take off, closely followed by the twins, then Fabian and Elsie. Barrington brought up the rear, and just when it looked as if he'd never get off the ground, his space hopper bounced on a sharp stone, punctured, and shot off into space.

Omonoslomo and Pickthank could only watch in amazement as within seconds he'd overtaken the others and narrowly missed a star bus coming in the opposite direction.

'What have I done?' wailed Omonoslomo, shaking his head. 'Those children couldn't guard a piggy bank, let alone a planet. When they arrive back on earth and take their special powder, their powers will start working and then goodness knows what might happen. The world will now be guarded by a bunch of idiots!'

Omonoslomo put his head wearily on Pickthank's shoulder and watched gloomily as the blur that was Barrington hurtled perilously towards earth like a pink and orange comet.

Four

'Seymour? Elsie? Is that you?' Mrs Potts called from the living room as Seymour and Elsie, followed by the others, sneaked in through the back door with their space hoppers under their arms.

The journey back to earth had been thrilling. It was surprising how many things there were to avoid in space, but by a stroke of luck they'd all managed to land safely in Seymour's next-door neighbour's garden. They'd flattened the rose bushes a bit, but at least they were all in one piece.

As they raced across the kitchen, Mrs Potts called out again.

'Won't be a minute, Mum,' shouted Seymour, hurrying everyone up the stairs.

'I'm just going to check on my ants.' He raced up after them and hustled them into his bedroom.

Seymour slammed the door behind him, and locked it.

'Phew! That was a close shave. I thought your mum was going to see us,' whispered Barrington, perching himself on the windowsill and resting his feet on his space hopper, which had by now lost half its air.

'I wish we could have stopped off at the launderette. I could have done a quick wash,' moaned Fabian, brushing some flecks of space debris from his suit.

Seymour looked around his room. Everything seemed to be as he'd left it. He glanced at his alarm clock. Four o'clock. No wonder his mum hadn't sounded worried – this was his usual time for getting home from school. He'd only left earth for about an hour and a half.

On his bed lay the tin of sweet wrappers

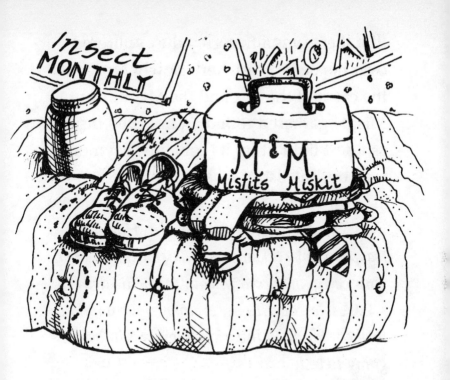

that he was collecting and next to it, folded
in a nice neat pile, was his school uniform.
On top of this was a yellow box with a
blue handle; printed on the side of it in
silver letters were the initials M M. This
was his Miskit.

Seymour stuffed the space hoppers into
the wardrobe and they all flopped down
on the bed. Although his school clothes
were remarkably clean, Seymour noticed

that there was a fine grey dust scattered over his bedspread. Very slowly he opened the catch of the box and the Magnificent Misfits gathered round and peeped inside as a soft light lit up its contents. Seymour read out the list of what it contained:

'1. One bottle of Power Powder. Half a teaspoon to be taken once a day sprinkled over your cereal or mixed in your favourite drink.

2. A telescope. To be set up by your window to check for alien invasion every night before going to bed.

3. A Slapper Blapper. A Machine that fires Glooch. This substance grows on Twart and is a cross between chewing gum and boiled spinach and smells like a pig's bedroom. Fire it in the face of your enemy and they'll be helpless for hours. The more they try to pull it off, the more attached it becomes. Handle with care.

4. Passport containing your new identity as a Magnificent Misfit This will enable you to travel freely around the universe.

5. A mobile phone. This is your means of communication and you can speak to your fellow Misfits four thousand light years away or just around the corner. The number is 10001.

6. A packet of plasters in case you fall over – it can be very dangerous being a superhero.

Good Luck. And may the Magnificence of the Misfits go with you!'

Just as Seymour closed the lid, there was a knock at his door.

'Seymour. What are you doing in there? Your tea's ready.' His mum rattled the door handle. Seymour leapt up and, putting a finger to his lips, motioned for everyone to crawl under the bed. Then he began to hurriedly scramble out of his suit. His mum knocked again.

'Seymour. Have you got someone in there?'

'No, Mum. Just me and my ants,' replied Seymour, struggling with the zip at the back. 'I bet Superman never has this trouble,' he mumbled, as he hopped around the room trying desperately to balance on one leg, the suit half on, half off. Suddenly he fell into a bedside lamp and sent it crashing.

'What on earth's going on?!' cried his mum, rattling the door handle again.

'It's OK. Everything's under control,' replied Seymour, finally escaping from his outfit, bundling it up and shoving it under his bed along with everyone else. Quickly putting on his dressing gown he opened the door. Mrs Potts stood there frowning at him. Then she peered over his shoulder.

'What's that box thing doing on your bed?' she asked, pointing to the Miskit.

'Oh, that's Barrington's lunchbox. He left it in my locker by mistake,' replied Seymour hastily. He glanced down at the bed. Barrington's big toe was sticking out. Seymour coughed loudly and the toe shot out of sight.

Mrs Potts stared at him, looking concerned. 'You're looking very pale, Seymour. You haven't been cooped up in the classroom all day, have you?'

'No, Mum. I've had plenty of fresh air,' replied Seymour, eyeing the space hoppers as they began to push open the wardrobe

door with a creak. 'That storm today has made me feel like a new person.' He smiled at his mum. 'In fact. I feel quite *magnificent*. Won't be long.' And he shut his door just as all the space hoppers came tumbling out of his wardrobe and bounced across the bedroom floor.

It was getting late and Seymour was absolutely exhausted. He lay in bed under his covers and dialled his friends on his Misfit mobile phone.

Everyone had arrived back home safely, though it had taken Barrington much longer as he had kept on flying in the wrong direction, and his space hopper was no longer working on full power. Also, Keith had had a bit of an accident with his Slapper Blapper and fired the thing at himself by mistake. It had taken him the best part of an hour to get it off in the bath and he'd had a *really* good moan about that, of course!

Eventually, Seymour said goodnight to everyone and wondered whether he'd wake up the next morning and find that it had all been an amazing dream.

However, just as he began to drift off, the phone rang under his pillow. Seymour fumbled for it and put it to his ear. It was Omonoslomo, calling all the way from the planet Twart.

'Are the pickled onions safe, Seymour Misfit?' he asked, his voice crackling and sounding far, far away.

'Yes, Omonoslomo,' replied Seymour. 'I've put them in my sock drawer.'

'Have you folded up your Misfit costume?'

Seymour peered under his bed and yawned. The outfit still lay in a bundle along with some odd socks, a half-eaten apple and a broken Gameboy. He really couldn't be bothered to move it now.

'Yes. It's neatly folded at the end of my bed,' he lied.

'Have you deflated your space hopper, Seymour?' asked Omonoslomo gravely. Seymour yawned again and nodded his head. He looked sleepily at the wardrobe and saw that one of the hopper's ears was sticking out of the door.

'Sure have,' he replied, settling comfortably down beneath the covers.

'But most importantly of all, Seymour,

have you checked through your telescope for alien invasion tonight?'

'Uh huh,' nodded Seymour, drifting happily off to sleep with Omonoslomo's voice now becoming a distant drone.

Seymour *hadn't* remembered to check through his telescope at all and neither had any of the others. If they had, they wouldn't have observed just the stars, and the moon, and the inky-blue sky. They would have seen a wild-eyed, rollerblading granny hitching a ride on top of a battered ice-cream van with big glass wings.

With her fox-fur streaming out behind her, Ma Vile screeched with delight as her loathsome grandson swerved the van from side to side trying to topple her off.

'You won't get rid of me that easily, sonny boy,' she cried, hoisting up her skirts and enjoying the ride.

Vince Vile stuck his head out of the window and shook his fist at her. 'Just you wait, you gruesome old crone. I'll lose you and your flea-bitten fox when we land,' he roared, as the Vile Van, headlights flashing and horn blaring, headed straight for planet earth . . .

Dream on, *Magnificent Misfits*. For tomorrow you take on *The Viles*!! Zzzzz.